For: Vicki, Lily, Edward and Tilly

Rockpool Children's Books
15 North Street
Marton
Warwickshire
CV23 9RJ

First published in Great Britain by Rockpool Children's Books Ltd. 2009
Text and Illustrations copyright ©Stuart Trotter 2009
Stuart Trotter has asserted the moral rights
to be identified as the author and illustrator of this book.
© Rockpool Children's Books Ltd. 2009

Printed in China

rockpool
children's books

Stuart Trotter
Polar White

It was snowing outside.

"A perfect day for the seaside,"
said Polar White to Rusky.
He packed his beach bag.
He had a bucket, a spade,
some sandwiches and a drink.

Rusky had his ball.

Polar White and little Ted got on
the sledge, and Rusky pulled them

– *whooshhh* –

across the snow!

They
swishhhhed
through an ice cave.

They
whooshhhed
down a snowy slope.

At the seaside, Polar White made a
snow castle. It wasn't very good.

Rusky tried to make a snow husky,
by rolling a large snowball!

Polar White took his boat
down to the seashore.
He knelt down and gazed
at his reflection
in the water.
Suddenly...

... **"Boo!"**
said Walter Walrus.
"Coming for a swim?"

Polar White hung on tight,
as Walter swam deep into the ocean,

through shoals of shiny, silvery fish...

...and alongside Harry the humpback whale!

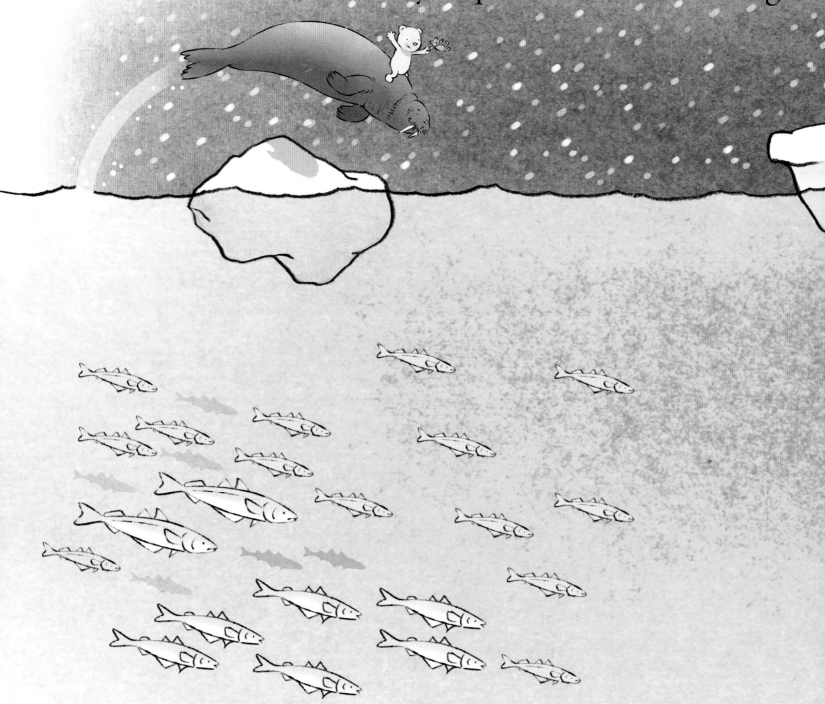

They leapt over a small iceberg...

...and swam under a huge one!

While Polar White and Ted got dry,
Walter took Rusky for a ride.
Rusky didn't like getting wet,
so he sat on Walter's head.
"Woo hoo!"
he whooped.

Their swim had made them all
very hungry, so they tucked into
Polar White's picnic.

"Yummy,"
munched Walter.

They waved goodbye to Walter
and got back on the sledge.
The swishing and swooshing of the sledge across
the snow made Polar White
fall fast asleep.

What a lovely day
they'd had at the seaside!

"Huh!
It might have been
a good day for some!"
thought a very
soggy Ted.